FOAL

Roland Wright

Brand-New Page

Don't miss these great books!

Roland Wright

Roland Wright
Brand-New Page

by Tony Davis
illustrated by Gregory Rogers

Delacorte Press

Text copyright © 2008 by Tony Davis
Illustrations copyright © 2008 by Gregory Rogers

All rights reserved. Published in the United States by Delacorte Press, an imprint of Random House Children's Books, a division of Random House, Inc., New York. Originally published in paperback by Random House Australia, Sydney, in 2008.

Delacorte Press is a registered trademark and the colophon is a trademark of Random House, Inc.

Visit us on the Web! www.randomhouse.com/kids

Educators and librarians, for a variety of teaching tools,
visit us at www.randomhouse.com/teachers

Library of Congress Cataloging-in-Publication Data
Davis, Tony.
Brand-new page / by Tony Davis ; illustrated by Gregory Rogers. —
1st American ed.
p. cm. — (Roland Wright ; #2)
Summary: In 1409, aspiring knight Roland Wright joins the royal household at
Twofold Castle as a new page, but his plan to impress King John and his knights
quickly backfires.
ISBN 978-0-385-73802-6 (trade) — ISBN 978-0-385-90707-1 (lib. bdg.) —
ISBN 978-0-375-89406-0 (ebook)
[1. Knights and knighthood—Fiction. 2. Castles—Fiction. 3. Middle Ages—
Fiction.] I. Rogers, Gregory, ill. II. Title.
PZ7.D3194Br 2009
[Fic]—dc22
2008053075

The text of this book is set in 16-point Bembo.

Book design by Michelle Gengaro

Printed in the United States of America

10 9 8 7 6 5 4 3 2 1

First American Edition

Contents

One

Twofold Castle

"Flaming catapults, Nudge, have you ever seen such a castle?"

The correct answer was "no." But because Nudge was a small white mouse, he couldn't say it.

Even if he could, the ten-year-old—well, almost-ten-year-old—redheaded boy who had asked the question was far too excited to wait for an answer.

"Imagine if there was a siege," Roland said as the pair looked up at King John's castle, an enormous stone fortress covering the entire top of the hill.

"Can't you just see hundreds of soldiers protecting the King, Nudge? Hundreds of archers shooting arrows from the battlements down onto the attackers . . . and soldiers pouring boiling oil on men charging at the drawbridge with a battering ram . . . and gallant knights swinging broadswords atop warhorses covered with shining armor."

As it turned out, Nudge couldn't see any of that. He stood on Roland's shoulder, sniffed the air with his pink nose and continued to look around. All he could see was a castle so quiet and peaceful it seemed almost to be sleeping under the blue summer sky. Nudge could hear birds singing and the sound of the wind rustling the leaves in the trees.

Roland, however, could hear the whoosh of spears, the shouting of soldiers, the snorting of horses waiting to charge.

He could smell flaming arrows hitting the wet leather that had been strung up to protect the siege towers from fire. He could feel the castle shuddering as boulders were slung into the walls by the most powerful catapult of all, the trebuchet.

Mind you, Roland had been daydreaming about such things for most of the two days he and his small group had been traveling. When Roland wasn't daydreaming, he was talking about all the things he would do and learn as a new page at the King's castle.

"I'll go to tournaments and see real jousting," he said to his taller, blond-haired brother, Shelby, as they walked along. "And I'll learn to ride horses and to hunt with falcons. I'm the luckiest boy in the whole world."

"You certainly are," said Shelby, still a little sad that his younger brother had been chosen ahead of him. "But I know you'll make the most of it."

"And Father," said Roland, "I'm going to be the best page, then the best squire, then the best knight. I know if I try hard enough I can be, and you'll be so proud of me. Especially when I wear armor made by you."

"I have abundant faith in you, Roland," said his father, flicking back his thick brown hair and kindly pretending that he hadn't heard Roland say the same thing again and again for two whole days. "You can do anything if you set your mind to it, son. You've already demonstrated that."

There was someone else Roland spoke to on the long journey to the King's castle from the small village where the Wright family lived: Sir Gallawood. He had offered to travel with the Wrights, as it could be a dangerous business walking through the woods in the year 1409. It could be dangerous doing many other things six centuries ago too, so it was always handy to take a knight in armor along with you.

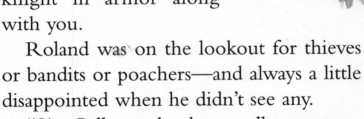

Roland was on the lookout for thieves or bandits or poachers—and always a little disappointed when he didn't see any.

"Sir Gallawood, please tell me more about King John . . . and his castle," said Roland as he walked alongside the knight's horse.

"Well, young Roland," said Sir Gallawood, "it's called Twofold Castle.

That's because it has double walls to make it even safer from attack. And there are many, many pages there, most of them sons of the most important men in the country." He let out a hearty laugh. "Well, the sons of the men who *think* they are the most important in the country."

Sir Gallawood looked down at Roland with a more serious expression. "Twofold Castle is a magnificent place. The finest horses are there, and the best squires and of course the bravest, most talented knights. I personally promised the King I would bring you safely to his castle to start your new life as a page."

"You've met the King!" Roland cried with glee.

"Yes, I—" Sir Gallawood started, but he was straightaway interrupted by Roland.

"Flaming catapults, Sir Gallawood, that's so exciting. I can't think of anything more wonderful than meeting the King, except fighting in a battle alongside him. What is he like?"

"King John is a fair and just man," said Sir Gallawood. "And now he has given you a chance that almost never comes to boys who aren't from noble families. Always remember: being a page is the first step to being a knight, but it is also about serving King John and his court. It will be a great honor to do that. You are a very lucky boy."

Sir Gallawood was right. Roland knew how fortunate he was. It wasn't just that the King's life had been saved by a suit of armor made by Roland's father. Nor was it that the King had offered to take in one of the armorer's sons as a way of saying thank you. The truly remarkable thing was that Roland had been chosen ahead of his brother, Shelby, who was already eleven.

Roland looked up at the walls and turrets of Twofold Castle and cried out, "We're here, Nudge! We're here!"

But sitting up on that huge hill, the castle was still half an afternoon's walk away. That was enough time for Roland to tell his father several more times that he was going to be the best page, then the best squire and then the best knight. It was also enough time to ask Sir Gallawood another thirty questions about life in a castle. And to daydream some more too.

When the small group finally arrived at the edge of the green moat that surrounded Twofold Castle, a sentry shouted from the top of the gatehouse. The large black drawbridge soon dropped and a man on

a beautiful white horse rode out to meet the newcomers.

"So, this is the leave-taking," sighed Roland's father.

"Ah, Sir Gallawood," said the man on the white horse, ignoring the others. His voice sounded like a big, rusty hinge being opened. It echoed around the hills.

"Yes, Constable," said Sir Gallawood, "I present to you a small and thin, but very, very brave young boy named Roland Wright."

Sir Gallawood dismounted and put his hand on Roland's shoulder. "And Roland, I present to you the King's constable, who is in charge of running the castle."

The constable was a mountain of a man. He wore a bright red surcoat with the royal crest on the front. He had the biggest, blackest mustache Roland had ever seen. His head was completely bald and shiny, but his eyebrows were almost as big, black and bushy as his mustache.

Roland couldn't see his eyes or his mouth through all the hair.

"I'm pleased to meet you, Sir Constable," Roland said, wondering where to look.

"Just call me Constable, and always do exactly as I tell you," came the reply from somewhere under the mustache. The voice was so low and creaky it made Roland's ears ache. "Now, let's hurry along."

Roland realized that after all the hours of traveling there wasn't going to be time to say goodbye properly. The constable was in a hurry, and Roland had to do exactly as he was told.

"Bye, Father, bye, Shelby," he blurted as the constable grabbed him by one arm, and Sir Gallawood grabbed him by the other, then helped prop him on the back of the constable's horse.

"We won't see you for at least a year, but we are confident you'll make us proud, son," Oliver Wright called as Roland found himself galloping across the drawbridge.

Roland was through the double walls of Twofold Castle and into the castle yard before he had time to wipe away the tears that were forming in his eyes. He didn't even look around at his new home. He just thought about how he no longer had his father and his brother by his side. The only friend at hand was Nudge, now safely in his small elm-wood box inside Roland's sack.

"Do you know what is expected of you

here, young man?" asked the constable loudly as he leapt off the horse and watched Roland fumble his way out of the saddle.

"Not completely," said Roland, who was still in shock and trying very hard to dry his eyes with his handkerchief while pretending to blow his nose. "But I am very keen to learn. I'm going to be the greatest knight in the world."

"They all say that," the constable rasped. "But most pages never even become squires, let alone knights. Some are sent home in the first week because they aren't right for the job.

"The only thing expected of you here, young Roland, is that you do exactly as you are told, and you speak to your betters only when asked a question. Do you understand that?"

"Yes, sir. I mean, yes, Constable."

"As we are busy because of the elephant, I'm going to ask—"

"The elephant?" Excitement raced back

into Roland's voice, but it quickly disappeared. The constable's huge eyebrows quivered and his shiny bald head reddened.

"I did not ask a question," he snapped. "You certainly have a lot to learn about how we do things here, young man."

At that point a boy ran up to the center of the courtyard where Roland and the constable were standing. He was nine or ten years old and was wearing the royal page uniform—a tunic with large red and blue squares, pulled tight by a thick black leather belt. The boy had curly yellow hair—the longest hair on a young boy Roland had ever seen.

"Humphrey," said the constable. "I want

you to take young Roland to his room so he can put his things down. Then I want you to look after him until it's time for him to join in the chores."

"Yes, Constable, yes, Constable." The boy seemed almost to dance as he talked—it was as if he couldn't stand still. Roland, who often had "hunches," decided straight-away that this boy with the long straw-colored hair was going to be a friend.

As the constable remounted his horse and rode away, Humphrey turned to Roland and smiled.

"Welcome to Twofold Castle, to Twofold Castle. We've all heard about you—the son of the famous armorer, the famous armorer. You are so lucky to be here right now. Tomorrow is going to be the most exciting day, the most exciting day for years."

Two

No Mice

"So this is the bailey," said Humphrey, still smiling, still dancing around—and still repeating his words. "The bailey, the bailey."

Thanks to Sir Gallawood, Roland already knew the bailey was the name for the main open area inside the castle walls. He had no idea, though, just how enormous the bailey in Twofold Castle would be.

There were people everywhere: walking from building to building, carrying food, carrying weapons, carrying buckets of water or rolling barrels of wine. People were leading horses, riding horses and even handfeeding horses in the long shadows made by the high stone walls. It was like the center of a very busy town, complete with a chapel at the northern end.

Humphrey started walking—almost skipping—toward a building next to the west wall. Roland followed. They went through a series of doors and corridors into a dark, damp-smelling room that was very small but very, very tall. Roland was sure it was three times as high as it was wide.

"This is our room," said Humphrey, with a huge grin. "You'll be sharing this with me and Morris, with me and Morris."

Roland opened his mouth but no sound came out.

"This will be yours," said Humphrey, pointing to a short, narrow bed. "The straw is a bit old but there are not too many bugs. Not too many bugs. You can put your things under it. Morris will be here later, here later."

"Oh!" said Roland, finding his voice again after the shock of seeing his room. "This is for me just until my proper bed is ready, is it?"

"I don't think so, don't think so," said Humphrey. "Why do you say that?"

"I thought in castles they had enormous beds of softest duck feather. That's what my brother, Shelby, told me."

"They probably do have enormous beds of softest duck feather—if you are the King or someone really important, really important. But if you are a page, or even a squire, you sleep on straw and eat in the servants' mess and do your toileting in one of the cold and windy garderobes, cold and windy garderobes, that hang over the moat."

"Urrgh!" said Roland.

"My father is a baron, a baron," said Humphrey, moving his weight from foot to foot, "and it's no different even for the son of a baron. But don't worry, we are going to have a lot of fun, a lot of fun, together."

Roland slumped down onto his bed and reached into his sack. He pulled out the small elm-wood box and opened it.

"What in heaven's name is that?"

shouted Humphrey as Roland held up Nudge.

Humphrey's question was so loud and sudden that Roland dropped the bag, the box—and the mouse.

"It's my pet," said Roland, scooping up the furry little white bundle and retrieving the box with a clatter and a thump. "Nudge. My littlest and best friend in the whole world. He brings me luck, too."

"Well, he has just brought you more luck. Bad luck. You are not allowed to have him here, have him here. The Queen is terrified of mice, terrified of mice. She hates them even more than she hates rats. And she hates rats more than she hates anything else in the world, anything else in the world. Except mice, of course."

"Oh," said Roland, nervously patting Nudge's head with his index finger. "I had no idea."

"Yes, Queen Margaret allows a slice of sugar cheese pie, of sugar cheese pie, to any page who hands in a dead mouse or rat to the constable. Once she had the King send his entire army through the castle trying to track down all the rodents. All the rodents."

"But this isn't a rodent. This is Nudge!"

"Either way, Nudge can't stay here," said Humphrey, shaking his head and making his long yellow hair swing around wildly. Humphrey had lost his smile but still seemed to be moving nervously whenever he spoke. "Anyway, it will scare away, scare away the elephant."

"Flaming catapults . . . the constable said something about an elephant. Do elephants really exist?"

"Oh, yes, oh, yes. The King has received one as a gift from King Notjohn. That's why tomorrow is the most exciting day, exciting day. The elephant will arrive and there will be a small festival."

"King Notjohn?" said Roland with surprise. There was just too much information.

"Yes, he is King John's twin brother. They looked so similar, the King and Queen named the firstborn John and the second Notjohn. John and Notjohn, Notjohn and John.

"John became King twenty years ago and made his brother the ruler of the conquered lands," Humphrey added. "And then, and then, a few months ago King John sent his brother a fine tapestry with a picture of an elephant on it. And now King Notjohn is sending back a real elephant. A real elephant. They are always trying to outdo each other."

Roland stroked Nudge's back with his middle finger. Nudge had a headache after being dropped. And he didn't like the cool, damp room Roland had brought him to. Nudge wished he could be shut back in his box and left alone.

"Who told you a mouse could scare an elephant?" Roland asked.

"The castle minstrel once sang a song about how the big elephant was scared by the tiny mouse, the tiny mouse," replied Humphrey, now smiling again. "There were all these rhymes about how the huge elephant *ran* twice as fast as a *man,* and at the squeak of a *mouse* it knocked down a *house,* and the people did *fuss* and the people did *frown* and so it was *thus* that they lost the whole *town.* He's a very clever, very clever, minstrel."

Roland was horrified. If he'd known mice weren't allowed in Twofold Castle he would have left Nudge with Shelby. He might even have stayed at home and let Shelby be the page.

"Look," said Humphrey. "I can see how fond you are, how fond you are, of this Nudge creature. Why don't you leave him in the box under your bed, and you can take some bread or cheese from the supper table to feed him. But by the new week, we'll have to work out what to do with him, do with him."

"Thank you so much, Humphrey," said Roland, but he wasn't much happier. Roland knew he couldn't just "do something" with Nudge. He had to keep his furry white friend with him. And he had to hope that a miracle happened before Monday; that if he was good enough, and did everything well enough, that somehow the King would allow Nudge to stay.

Humphrey was still talking. He was now explaining that the King had given the pages a holiday on the festival day, and this meant they could go to the open meadow in the morning.

"We'll be able to play with our swords before the elephant arrives. And on Monday, after we've worked out what to do with the mouse, to do with the mouse, you'll receive your page uniform and you'll join us at classes. Can you read?"

"No."

"Can you play a musical instrument?"

"No."

"Oh, well, it will be Lady Mary's job to teach you to play the lute and to know your manners. Know your manners. I suppose you don't know anything about falconry either, or horse riding, or how to play chess, or how to carve meat for the nobility. You have a lot to learn, a lot to learn."

"Yes, but I want to learn it all. I want to be a great page, and the world's greatest knight."

"They all say that," said Humphrey. "But maybe you will be, maybe you will be. Anyway, now it's time for the main meal. I must go and serve but I will collect you afterward, collect you afterward, and we shall have our supper in the servants' mess."

"Just one thing before you go, Humphrey."

"Yes, yes, Roland?"

"You wouldn't tell anyone about Nudge, would you? Not for a piece of sugar cheese pie? You won't even tell Morris, will you?"

"Of course I won't, of course I won't. I don't even like sugar cheese pie. And you don't need to worry, don't need to worry about Morris. He tells a few stories . . . well, if truth be told, he tells a lot of stories. He just doesn't know when to shush up. But he's nice enough. Nice enough.

"No, Roland, it's Hector you should watch out for. He's twelve years old and the meanest page in the castle. The meanest, meanest, meanest. Stay right out of his way."

Three

Hector

Roland sat waiting in his new bed-
room, watching Nudge pace up
and down his arm. Nudge looked
very ill at ease.

"Don't worry, Nudge,
I'll look after you," said
Roland, who was every
bit as uncomfortable
and wished he too
had an arm to
walk up and down.

What's more, Roland had been scratching his neck and head ever since Humphrey had mentioned bugs.

"   ," said Nudge nervously.

"Yes, I know," replied Roland, just as nervously.

After what seemed like a very long time, Roland heard footsteps and quickly put Nudge back into the small elm-wood box and slid it under his bed.

Humphrey pushed open the door. "I have done my chores, done my chores. We're off to eat, so follow me."

Humphrey ran down a series of corridors. With his bright mop of hair shaking from side to side, Humphrey skipped and swerved and shimmied as Roland followed.

They went up stairs, they went down stairs, they turned left, they turned right. There were so many twists and corners Roland was sure he would never find his way back if he ever had to do it on his own.

Finally they arrived in a large dining room filled with noisy people. There was a table of boys, thirty or more, all in red and blue pages' tunics. There was a table of squires, too, and rows of chambermaids and washerwomen and laborers.

Everyone was eating lumps of rough bread with slabs of cheese and small portions of salted fish. They washed it down with watery ale served in wooden bowls.

"Roland, this is someone you need to

meet," said Humphrey. "This is our room-mate, our roommate, Morris."

"Hello, Roland," said Morris, whose plump face produced two big dimples when he smiled. "I've heard about you. And have you heard about the elephant?"

"Only a little bit."

Morris ran his hand through his straight black hair and then rubbed his mouth with the back of his hand. "You know that an elephant is taller than a castle, don't you? And the gift may not be an elephant at all. I've heard that they are just saying it is an elephant."

"What else could it be?" asked Roland, a little unsure of himself.

Morris ran his hand back through his hair and across his mouth again. "It could be a griffin, that's what I've heard. A griffin has the head of an eagle and the body of a lion and the tail of a serpent. And it likes nothing better than to eat young boys."

Roland thought a griffin sounded even more exciting than an elephant—as long as it didn't come too close. He had only just begun to eat his bread and had taken only one sip of his ale when the constable walked in and said with his big, raspy voice: "Roland Wright!"

"Yes?" Roland answered softly. He wondered whether he was in trouble already. Maybe he wasn't sitting correctly, or wasn't eating in the proper way. Maybe he was spitting on the wrong part of the floor, or maybe the problem was that he was wiping his greasy hands on his shirt, instead of on his trousers like the other boys. He had a lot to learn about manners.

"Come with me," said the constable impatiently. He quickly led Roland down another series of corridors. As they walked, the constable talked through his

thick mustache and Roland realized he wasn't in trouble.

"I've been asked to take you to meet Lady Mary, young man," the constable said. He was speaking just as sternly as if Roland was in trouble. "You will be her special page. In return, it will be her job to teach you genteel manners and culture, which, by the look of you, will be no easy task."

There were more stairs and more corridors before Roland was pushed into the castle's Great Hall. It was an enormous room filled with tapestries and shields and long benches. There were noblemen standing around talking and noblewomen sitting in high-backed chairs doing fine needlework.

"I'm Lady Mary," one of the women said to Roland. She wore a bright blue dress with gold braiding and had an unusual pointed wimple on her head. "And you must be Roland Wright."

"Yes, Lady, ma'am, Mrs. . . . Mary," said Roland as he looked up at her face. He could tell straightaway that Lady Mary was gentle and kind. She spoke beautifully and had a lovely smile. Her skin was the color of bone; she was a real lady who had never been outside without shading her face.

"I will be teaching you all sorts of things, Master Wright. And I will be setting you special chores from the start of next week. I'm pleased to meet you, but I won't keep you from your supper any longer. You may go now."

"Thank you, my lady," said Roland, who moved toward the door and wondered how on earth he would find his way back. Just as he was leaving, Lady Mary spoke again. "Do you know your way to the servants' mess?"

"Yes, of course," Roland said. He didn't want to appear stupid.

"All the same," said Lady Mary, "I'll send one of my ladies-in-waiting with you, just to make sure."

Roland sighed with relief. He knew already that Lady Mary was one of the nicest women he had ever met. Best of all, under her pointed wimple Roland could see strands of bright red hair. He was very glad that Lady Mary was "his" lady.

When Roland returned to the servants' mess, he discovered that someone had eaten his bread, cheese and salted fish. His ale was gone too.

"How was your food?" asked a small page with brown hair that curved up at the ends like a helmet. He was licking his lips.

"Oh," said Roland with disappointment, "I suppose the little bit that I ate was

very good. Luckily, I already pock—"
Roland suddenly stopped talking.

"Sorry?" said the page with the helmet hair. Roland had been about to say "Luckily, I already pocketed something for Nudge before I left," but he remembered at the last moment that mice were forbidden.

Roland thought he should talk about something else, and do it quickly. "I didn't know we'd have bread and salted fish. I thought we'd have cockentrice—you know, that meal where the cook takes a half of two different animals and sews them together to create a new one and then roasts it."

Roland could hear boys laughing right along the table. He started to turn red. "What's so funny? When the King sent his men to congratulate my father, the officer-of-arms brought us a cockentrice. It had the head and wings of a rooster and the body of a suckling pig and all types of herbs and fruits inside it and it was the sweetest food I'd ever tasted. I thought in castles they ate cockentrice every night."

There was more laughter, until the helmet-haired boy rudely spat out a sentence. "Even in the King's castle you'll see a cockentrice only at a banquet—and the pages certainly don't eat any of it."

"Yes, yes," said Humphrey in a much kinder tone. "You are very lucky to have tasted one, tasted one. I'm surprised the King sent one outside the castle."

"Yes," hissed a boy with dark, bushy hair and sharp blue eyes, "and to a lowly household like yours!"

Roland was shocked by how rude this boy was—and by how ugly he was. He had a big mouth that stuck out of his face and a short, sloping forehead. Roland wasn't only shocked, he was angry.

"There's nothing lowly about my household," said Roland through clenched

teeth. "My father is a fine man, and so is my brother, Shelby. How dare you say otherwise."

When Roland started talking, everyone else went quiet except for Humphrey, who whispered in Roland's ear, "Be careful, be careful, that's Hector, Hector!"

All that could be heard elsewhere on the table were a few boys moving their spoons.

"Don't talk to me like that," Hector

snarled at Roland. When Hector breathed in between words he made a hissing noise like a snake— "s-s-s-s."

Hector stood up and showed himself to be a head and shoulders taller than Roland—and wider and heavier too. "Or should I say, s-s-s-s, don't talk to me like that unless you want your head knocked off, you ugly little poor boy, s-s-s-s, you redheaded squirt."

As he spoke, Hector grabbed a piece of bread from another boy's plate, chewed it a few times and threw the rest on the floor. The boy whose food had been taken didn't complain—even when Hector grabbed the boy's bowl, took a gulp of his ale and then splashed the rest on the table in front of Roland.

"My father owns thousands of acres," Hector said as he threw the boy's ale bowl over his shoulder, "and I can never be sent home because my father has his own army, s-s-s-s, and is so powerful the King needs him. He is almost as important as the King himself.

"You can be sent home, though. And believe me, you redheaded squirt, *s-s-s-s,* no tiny little poor boy will wear the page uniform while I'm here."

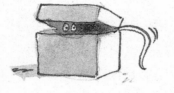

Four

One Thousand and One Knights

The day was almost over. Roland rubbed his empty, rumbling stomach and looked at his narrow bed. It wasn't filled with softest duck feathers. It was filled with soggy straw, and even fluffing it up with his hands didn't make it very soft.

No cockentrice to eat, no soft, wide bed to lie on—and a very scary boy named Hector to deal with. At least he had Lady Mary, who he hoped would look after him, and two roommates who seemed friendly. And at least he had managed to feed Nudge without Morris seeing, and had now pushed his box safely under the bed.

"When will I meet the knights?" Roland asked the other two boys as he climbed onto his straw and pulled up the blanket against the cold air of the tall, stone-walled room.

"Most of the knights are away at a tournament," Humphrey replied. "It's been so peaceful lately, peaceful lately, that the King has allowed them to go. The Queen has gone to cheer them. Cheer them. You won't be seeing any of them for a fortnight or more."

"It's a shame that it's peaceful," replied Roland. "I was hoping for a siege or two, or maybe a major battle."

"Don't you complain," replied Humphrey, now yawning loudly. "I've been waiting the whole year I've been here, the whole year, and there hasn't even been a single attack on the castle. Anyway, it's been a long day, a long day, and I'm going to go to sleep straighta . . . w . . . a . . ."

Roland could hear Humphrey sliding into a deep slumber before he even finished the sentence. Within a few seconds, Humphrey was pushing out huge grunting snores that sounded like stone houses falling down.

Ng-g-g-g-g-u-u-r-ch! Ng-g-g-g-g-u-u-r-ch!

"Humphrey is the noisiest sleeper in the known world," said Morris, rubbing his mouth with the back of his hand. He leaned over and blew out the last candle in the room. "But you'll get used to it. And you'll enjoy meeting the knights in two weeks."

"I've only met one knight," said Roland in the darkness. "Do you know Sir Gallawood?"

Ng-g-g-g-g-u-u-r-ch! Ng-g-g-g-g-u-u-r-ch!

Morris didn't reply until Humphrey's snore finally finished. "Of course I do, but he's not really interesting at all."

"I think he is," said Roland. "And Sir Gallawood is the best fighter I've ever seen, too."

"Oh, yes? Just wait until you see Sir Horridhead in action."

"Sir Who?"

"Sir Horridhead. He's so ugly that if he is losing a fight he can whip off his helmet and scare his opponent almost to death— even if the man isn't afraid of swords, axes or maces."

Ng-g-g-g-g-u-u-r-ch! Ng-g-g-g-g-u-u-r-ch!

"And there's Sir Flab," Morris continued, "a knight who eats so much he has to have leather straps with buckles at the back of his armor so it can stretch out to fit in his enormous gut."

"Flaming catapults . . ."

"Oh, yes," said Morris. "I remember a fight when Sir Flab thrust once with his sword, then once with his shield. When that didn't work he swung his huge belly around and knocked the other knight head over heels."

"Morris?"

"Yes?"

"Is there really a Sir Flab?" Roland was afraid he was being rude, but wasn't at all sure what to believe.

"Oh, yes. His first wife, Lady Evenflabbier, actually exploded during a festival. One minute she was saying 'Pass me another leg of lamb and a hogshead of ale.' The next moment, the leg of lamb and the hogshead of ale were going past me in the other direction at the speed of a cannonball."

Ng-g-g-g-g-u-u-r-ch! Ng-g-g-g-g-u-u-r-ch!

"It was very ugly," added Morris quietly in the darkness. "Sir Flab was so surprised he could scarcely eat another pig."

Roland was amazed by the story of Sir Flab and Lady Evenflabbier. And he was astounded by the way Humphrey's snores seemed to be getting even louder and closer together.

Ng-g-g-g-g-u-u-r-ch! Ng-g-g-g-g-u-

u-r-ch! Ng-g-g-g-g-u-u-r-ch! Ng-g-g-g-g-u-u-r-ch!

"Who is the champion knight?" Roland asked Morris when it was quiet again.

"The bravest, strongest, most handsome knight is Sir Smellalot. He is the King's best friend, too."

"Sir Smellalot?" Roland laughed out loud. "Why is he called that? Does he stink like a pongy pile of rubbish?"

"He is called Smellalot, Roland, simply because he can smell a lot. He detects things with his nose that other people can't. One of his best forms of defense is that he can sniff out danger."

"But it's a pretty silly name," said Roland, still unsure about what he was hearing. "Isn't it?"

Morris huffed. "They said that about Sir Dumdum and Sir Dogsbreath."

The stories kept coming. Morris was now talking about a knight who was only as tall as a squirrel and attacked the knees of other knights. But Roland could feel himself drifting away into sleep.

The last sound Roland heard was *Ng-g-g-g-g-u-u-r-ch! Ng-g-g-g-g-u-u-r-ch!*

When he woke at first light, Roland could hear Morris talking. He wondered if he had been talking all night. Then he heard Humphrey too—and this time Humphrey was talking, not snoring.

"No chores this morning, this morning," shouted Humphrey as he bounced around with delight and beamed a huge smile. "We're going to the meadow outside the north wall to practice fighting, practice fighting. Then this afternoon we'll see the elephant—or whatever the mystery beast is.

"You're so lucky, Roland, to be here now, to be here now. I'll find you a wooden sword."

The three boys ran to the servants' mess, ate bread and drank some more watery ale to break their fast, then walked out over the drawbridge and around to the meadow. Before they left, Roland had leaned over the side of his bed and quietly whispered.

"Sorry, Nudge, I must leave you in your box for the moment. I can't let anyone else know you are here. I'll bring you some food back, I promise."

When the boys arrived at the meadow carrying their wooden weapons, there

were other pages already paired off. They were fighting with fast, loud swipes of their swords. Only one boy was not joining in. He was the tallest there and Roland recognized him right away. The boy strode toward Roland and yelled straight into his face.

"Aha! Here's the one I've been waiting for. It's the new page, *s-s-s-s*, the dirty and poor boy."

"I'm not dirty and I'm not poor," said

Roland, but his voice sounded small and shaky. Hector looked even bigger, stronger and uglier in the daylight than he had at supper. Roland could feel his knees knocking together.

Humphrey tried to help. "Please leave him alone, Hector, we are here to sword fight and have fun, sword fight and have fun."

Hector let out a cruel laugh. "Shut up, Humphrey Humphrey."

Hector turned back toward Roland. "Not poor? How many thousands of acres of land does your father have, s-s-s-s, how many horses, how many houses?"

"He has one house. Nobody needs more than—"

"Just as I thought—you're a peasant. A lowly peasant. Just like your father and your father's father, s-s-s-s, and your father's father's father before him."

Roland's knees weren't knocking together anymore. He was too angry. "Go

away! Get away from me, you *ignoramus*."

Roland had no idea how the word "ignoramus" suddenly found its way into his sentence. It must have been one of the long words his father used. The word had just arrived from nowhere and seemed so right that Roland repeated it.

"Ignoramus! Go away!"

Humphrey and Morris gasped. Unlike Roland, they'd been to classes. They knew that "ignoramus" meant a stupid person, an idiot, a dunce, a complete dizzard. Nobody had ever talked to Hector like this before—and certainly not twice in two sentences.

"I'm not going anywhere," snarled Hector, his blue eyes glittering. "I'm going to fight you now because I'm the oldest page. I will be a squire soon and, *s-s-s-s*, it's my duty to give a thrashing to the new pages. It's the only way to show them what a real page should be able to do.

"And it will give me great pleasure to thrash a little squirt with red hair, *s-s-s-s*. A squirt who is here only because his father bends old metal."

"He doesn't bend old metal," said Roland. His voice was much stronger now. "My father is the finest armorer in the land, and he uses only the best steel. He can stamp By Royal Appointment on his armor because he saved the King's life."

Just as Roland said that, Hector rushed at him, swinging his wooden sword wildly, and talking and hissing at the same time, too.

"That's rubbish, poor boy, *s-s-s-s*. It's God who looks after the King. The King doesn't need the help of peasants, and neither does a person like my father."

Hector was stronger and faster than Roland expected. And because he was so much taller his sword seemed to be coming down from way above Roland's head.

"You'll be gone in a week, you squirt, *s-s-s-s,* just like Percival and Lucas and Gwayne and all those other silly little poor boys the King tried to improve. You can't improve peasants. They'll always be smelly and stupid."

Between these words, Roland blocked—left, right, center—with such speed that even Hector was surprised. But when their swords were locked, Hector suddenly pushed his shield forward as hard as he could, whacking Roland right across the side of the face.

It was a horrible blow. Roland found himself lying on the ground. Hector's sword was held on high, about to come crashing down.

Five

The Elephant

Hector's sword fell hard and fast, but Roland somehow managed to slide out of the way and get back to his feet.

Hector started slicing at Roland's head and body even more fiercely. But if there was one thing Roland could do, it was move his sword quickly. Back home he had practiced for hours by throwing an acorn against the side of the village well and swiping it with his sword no matter which way it bounced.

Now, with his bottom lip stuck out, his eyes locked in concentration and his face still throbbing from the blow with the shield, Roland lifted his weapon quickly as Hector swung left. Their swords smashed together.

Hector swung right but Roland had his sword in place again. And when Hector put all his strength into a stab toward Roland's stomach, the brand–new page swiped down so quickly it stopped the sword on the spot and sent a shock wave right up Hector's arm.

"Ouch!" cried Hector as his face crunched up in pain. "That was nothing to do with you, poor boy," he quickly added. "I just twisted my ankle, *s-s-s-s,* in a rabbit hole."

Roland knew he had to keep blocking or he would be horribly hurt. Hector was every bit as strong as he was nasty.

"You know I'm only warming up, poor boy. And when I'm warmed up, *s-s-s-s,* I'll have you chopped into little pieces."

If Hector wasn't already warmed up, Roland wondered why his face was bright red and why his bushy black hair was filled with sweat.

Hector slashed and swiped but he still couldn't find a way through. Roland had now learned to stay away from the shield and he could sense that Hector was tiring and becoming slower.

Roland didn't feel in danger anymore. Although he wasn't as strong as Hector, he was quicker. Everything that Roland had picked up in days and weeks of sword fighting with his brother, Shelby, was now helping him. Roland was so glad he had an older brother.

But Roland was just as hot and tired as Hector and didn't know what else to do except to keep blocking. There were a couple of moments when he saw a gap and could have attacked and struck Hector. But he was worried that beating Hector might make for even bigger problems. Roland had to keep defending instead and hope that something would happen to end the fight peacefully.

But the fight kept going on, and on, and on, and on. Roland and Hector slashed their wooden swords noisily and pushed each other forward and backward across the meadow, both growing more and more exhausted. All the other boys had stopped to watch—and to wonder how it was all going to finish.

Ding! Ding! A loud bell sounded from within the castle and suddenly Hector dropped his sword and shield. "That's for me," he said. "I have to help with the horses. I'll beat you later, *s-s-s-s,* you little squirt. You're not even worth the trouble now."

Hector turned and walked away, though not before swinging his right boot and catching Roland just above the knee.

Roland fought back tears as he rubbed

his thigh and watched Hector walk away. The other boys waited until Hector had disappeared around the corner of the castle wall before they ran up.

"Well done, Roland," said one.

"I've never seen anyone move his sword so quickly," added another.

"That showed him," the boy with the helmet hair said. "He didn't really have to help with the horses. That bell was for the guards."

"If the King saw you fight like that," Humphrey said, putting his hand on Roland's shoulder, "he'd make you a knight, make you a knight, straightaway."

"The only bad thing," said Morris, "is that Hector is going to be really angry now. You've hurt his pride and so you'll have to watch yourself very carefully. Let's hope it's a griffin that we see this afternoon—and that it eats him."

When Roland walked back to his room, he leaned down under the bed.

"What a morning, Nudge. I knew it was going to be tough fitting in with the children of the rich and noble, but I didn't know it would be this tough."

Roland flipped the top of the box and lifted Nudge out. In the dampness of the room Roland suddenly let loose an enormous sneeze—all over Nudge.

"Sorry!"

"Yuck!" thought a very wet and sticky Nudge as Roland pushed him into his top pocket.

"If I take you with me to see the elephant—or whatever the mystery animal is—will you promise to be very still and quiet?"

"   ," Nudge replied grumpily.

"You can't dress like that, can't dress like that, in front of the King," Humphrey said, looking over Roland's tatty clothes. "Wear this spare surcoat. Put it over your tunic, over your tunic. It's even the right colors."

It wasn't a proper uniform, and it was a bit too big, but Roland still felt proud wearing the same red and blue squares as the other pages as they all stood in the bailey waiting for the mystery creature.

"Here it is!" screamed the page with the helmet hair. Sure enough, soon they all could see a strange beast being marched across the drawbridge. A large man in a black leather coat carried a whip in one hand and a leash in the other. Tumblers and

jugglers rolled head over heels and threw volleys of jingling balls high into the air. A minstrel dressed in almost every color Roland had ever seen, and with bells on his hat and shoes, plucked a small stringed instrument and sang a funny song in a high voice.

"A present, a present
King Notjohn of East
Has sent us a marvelous
Huge-normous beast."

The animal was an elephant, not a griffin, though since Roland had never seen either, he had to take other people's word

for it. Whatever it was, it was the most extraordinary animal he had ever cast his eyes on.

"Flaming catapults, Nudge," Roland said to his top pocket. "You'll have to stay hidden, but I can tell you it's got a huge tail on its nose and another little one at the other end. And its front tail almost reaches the ground . . . and it has a mouth at the top of it . . . a mouth at the top of its tail!

"It has got skin like dry mud, too, and ears like huge leaves of gray lettuce, and there are two great big white spears sticking out the sides of its face. It's not taller than a castle like Morris said, but it is still very, very big. . . ."

A flurry of trumpets sounded and two long rows of guards appeared. King John walked between them and up a set of stairs to a small stage. It was the first time Roland had seen the King. He was tall and bearded and looked very kingly in his red, blue and gold coat and with his large silver crown studded with jewels. The King greeted the crowd, and Roland decided that he sounded very kingly too.

"For many years we've heard about elephants," King John said in a strong, regal voice. "The Romans brought many of them to Europe fifteen hundred years ago, but now there are only a few, and most of them are owned by kings. Like all of you today, I have only seen elephants in drawings, paintings and tapestries. It is a great pleasure and the cause of much excitement to see one in the flesh."

There was not a sound made anywhere while the King spoke, except by the short, fat man who stood right next to him on the stage. This man kept producing little coughs as if he wanted to be noticed.

"I'm told this elephant weighs as much as fifty men," explained the King, "and its long nose, which is called the trunk, can be used to pick things up, or to suck up liquids so that they can be pumped into the elephant's mouth. The blades on its face are called tusks and are made of a beautiful material called ivory."

As the King spoke, the elephant slowly folded its trunk back to wipe its eyes and scratch its neck. People gasped. It was like no living thing they had ever seen.

"And despite its size, I am told by my brother King Notjohn that it is a gentle animal, as long as it is given the right food—and plenty of it. It can eat five hundred pounds of grass, grain, fruits and nuts in a single day. That's the weight of a small horse."

When the King finished his speech he walked off the stage. Roland noticed that the short man followed the King very closely, almost step for step. The short man had a huge stomach and was expensively dressed. He wore a fancy armored breastplate featuring an elaborate coat of arms. He carried a knight's sword on his belt.

"Maybe that's Sir Flab, Nudge," Roland whispered to his top pocket.

Everyone in the castle, including the King and "Sir Flab," watched as the handler in the leather coat walked the elephant around the square. As it moved, everything swung from side to side—its trunk, its stomach, its ears and its tail.

After four laps of the bailey, the handler led the elephant toward a special pen that had been built for it. When the handler pulled the leash toward the pen and gave the elephant a couple of very gentle slaps with the whip, the animal lifted its trunk and let out a sound like a short blast from a hundred trumpets. Everyone grabbed their ears and wondered what would happen next, but the elephant slowly and peacefully moved into the pen.

The handler pulled a big wooden door across the front of the pen, slid an iron-

covered beam in front of it, then dropped a small bolt into an eyelet at the top, so the beam couldn't slide back out. The elephant looked back over the barrier with big, sad eyes.

Roland stood watching and daydreaming as the King left the bailey and the crowd began to break up. Roland was thinking of how lucky he was, and wishing he could share this moment with Shelby— and his father, whose cleverness had got him here in the first place.

Roland imagined King John walking up to the three of them, shaking their hands, thanking them for coming, and inviting them in for a special feast—with a cockentrice, of course. He imagined the King telling the whole royal household how clever and talented the Wrights were, and then making his father a baron. But halfway through the daydream, Roland was jostled from behind and heard a voice just near his left ear.

"You've been here yesterday and today, poor boy, *s-s-s-s*. That's two days too many as far as I'm concerned. But I've worked it all out. You'll be on your way home tomorrow, *s-s-s-s*."

Six

Lord Urbunkum

Roland walked slowly across the bailey and leaned against the eastern wall. He was sweating and feeling quite uncomfortable.

"How am I going to deal with Hector?" he asked his top pocket. When he looked up, Roland saw "Sir Flab" walking toward him.

"You must be the new page," the man said. He had a strange voice. It was loud and high-pitched and it echoed, as if an

even smaller man was inside him shouting to be heard. "Son of an armorer?"

"Yes, son of Oliver Wright. I'm Roland." The man really did have adjustable leather straps on the back of his fancy breastplate.

"You must be very pleased to meet me," said the man. "I'm sure you know I'm Urbunkum—Lord Urbunkum. But feel free to call me 'Your Most Gracious and Worthy Honor.'"

"Yes, er, Your Most Gracious and Worthy Honor." Roland was very pleased the man had given his name. Otherwise he might have said "You must be Sir Flab."

Lord Urbunkum had small eyes that were far apart and a round red face covered with blotches. He had only a tiny amount of hair, just a little clump above each ear and a third clump on top of his forehead. He said in a very serious voice, "I suppose you are wondering what a man as important as me does, page boy."

"Well, I wasn't," replied Roland. "But I will now, Sir . . . Lord . . . Gracious Honor . . . Mister . . . Urbunkum."

"I train the knights, that's what I do," the short man yelped with pride. "I sit them down and tell them all the ways they can be better in battles and jousts and every other part of their lives."

"Flaming catapults," said Roland. He was now very excited, having almost forgotten about the Hector problem. "You teach the other knights how to fight! You must be so clever. . . . You must be the greatest knight. You must have won huge jousting competitions and fought in great battles, and won them all."

"No, no," said Lord Urbunkum in a slightly lower tone, as if Roland had said something very silly. "I've never fought anyone and, luckily, I've never been in battles. Awful things, battles. No, Master Wright, I'm instead what we call an expert."

Roland was confused. "But why would someone who fights in battles need to be told how to do it by someone who doesn't fight in battles?"

"Oh, dear, dear, dear," said Lord Urbunkum in the same tone, as if Roland had again said something silly. Or trodden in something smelly.

"It is very important, Master Wright, that an expert like myself has no practical experience of any kind. That way he can look at a problem from a fair and neutral point of view, and come up with a series of easy-to-remember slogans about the best way to solve it."

Roland was still confused. He put his hand over his chest, just in case Lord Urbunkum saw Nudge moving.

"Can you read, Master Wright?"

"No," Roland replied. "Not yet. But I will learn."

"If you want to become a great knight, you must learn to read. Otherwise you won't be able to study my books. There's *You Can Be a Winner: The Seven Secrets of Sword Fighting,* for a start, and *Damsel in Distress: A Rescuer's Guide.* I've just finished one about dragons."

"You've seen a dragon?" Roland yelled with amazement. "Flaming cata— Well, fry my gizzards, that's so incredible. What do they—"

"Don't be silly, boy," Lord Urbunkum replied with a voice that made Roland again worry that he'd trodden in something. "Very few people have ever seen a dragon, and none of them have my expert background. But if *you* ever see a dragon,

Master Wright, you'll do well to have read my book first.

"His Majesty King John thinks *Slay a Dragon a Day* is such a useful book he is paying the monks to write out a second copy. Maybe even a third, so that more knights can read it at the same time. I'm working with the monks on some new pictures so we can show exactly what a dragon looks like and how best to smite it."

Just as Lord Urbunkum said the words "smite it," there was a giant scream from the other side of the bailey.

The scream was followed by shouting and yelling, then the crashes and thuds of big things being knocked over. It sounded like a battle, or at least what Roland imagined a battle would sound like. Maybe there was a siege at last!

"Don't panic, don't panic," a man yelled over the din. But even he was panicking. And so was everyone else.

Roland was pleased he was standing

next to an expert, someone who would know exactly what to do. He looked carefully at His Most Gracious and Worthy Honor. Lord Urbunkum's eyes seemed to become even smaller and farther apart. His red skin became redder, the blotches on his face turned whiter.

"You'd better check everything is all right, page boy," Lord Urbunkum said as he turned quickly to walk through a nearby doorway. "I have some urgent business to attend to."

Seven

The Great Escape

Roland looked across the bailey and quickly realized what the trouble was: the elephant was on the loose. The bashing and thumping noises hadn't been caused by the elephant, though. They were the sounds of people knocking things over as they screamed and ran away.

Roland took several paces forward and looked at the elephant, which was now standing still and shaking. He decided it

was more scared than any of the people watching it. But Roland didn't want to get too close, nevertheless. The elephant took a few small steps toward a group of people trapped up against a wall, then stopped and looked at them.

"Maybe it won't hurt anyone," said one man as the crowd started to calm down.

"I think it should be shot with arrows, just in case," said another.

"Where is the handler?" asked a third.

"I know," said a fourth. "One of the older pages told him he had to report to the King immediately."

Roland looked into the elephant's big, wrinkly eyes and knew King John was right—it was a gentle beast. Nobody should shoot it with arrows. They just needed to find the handler.

After a while the elephant began slowly wandering around the bailey, swinging its trunk and occasionally letting out the sort of low grumble a dog would make—if the dog was the size of a small house. At times it flapped its big lettuce leaf ears as if it was a bird trying to take off.

The elephant walked behind a row of wooden wine barrels and made another colossal trumpeting sound with its trunk.

Then it stayed perfectly still, looking at everyone and breathing heavily.

The constable stepped forward and, in his loud, raspy voice, ordered everyone to stand behind the thick wooden wall that surrounded the chapel. "And does anyone know who opened the gate to the elephant's pen?" he bellowed, scratching his bald head.

"I do!" yelled someone running out of the crowd. "It was Roland, *s-s-s-s,* the new page."

The constable's bushy eyebrows lifted with surprise. "Why would he do that?"

"Because . . . because . . . he's poor," said Hector with another hiss or two. "These things happen when you try to make a knight, or even a page, out of a poor boy, *s-s-s-s.*"

Roland couldn't believe what he was hearing. "It's not true, it's not true, I didn't do it," he said, but his tiny voice was drowned out by the crowd that had gathered around him.

"You let him out?" a woman snarled.

"We could all have been killed," said an old man. "We still might be."

"I wouldn't like to be you right now, young page," said an even older man.

The constable grabbed Roland roughly by the sleeve and walked him out of the bailey, up a set of stairs and along a corridor.

"We've got other things to deal with right now, so you can wait," the constable

barked as he pushed Roland into a small stone lockup.

He then turned an enormous key in the lock of the thick wooden door. "I'll be back, young man. There will be an inquiry. I wouldn't like to be you right now, either."

Roland had never felt so scared and lonely in his life.

"Why don't they believe me?" Roland asked as he lifted Nudge out of his top pocket. "I had no reason to let the elephant out."

The lockup had no furniture and only

one tiny window near the ceiling. Roland bent down to sit on the floor.

"You are the only friend I've got here, Nudge. And even if I get out of this room, I've told Humphrey we'd somehow get you out of the castle by the new week. What are they going to do to us? What is my father going to say?"

As Roland sat on the cold stone he felt a lump in the side pocket of his tunic. He stuck his hand in and pulled out a short, thick iron stick. He had no idea what it was or where it came from, but he had more important things on his mind. Roland put the small piece of iron straight back into his pocket, sat down and started rubbing Nudge's neck. He could still hear a great deal of noise from out in the bailey.

Nudge looked at Roland carefully, then

twitched his pink nose, stood up on his rear legs and lifted his eyes up toward the window. He sniffed the air and then reached up toward the small square of light with his right front paw.

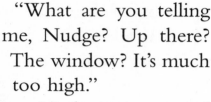

"What are you telling me, Nudge? Up there? The window? It's much too high."

Nudge now seemed to be pointing at the window with both front paws.

Roland looked carefully at Nudge. "Really? Do you think it is possible?"

Roland still thought it was too high but he knew that if he only had one friend left, he should do what that one friend wanted. He should try to climb up to the window. Roland put Nudge back in his pocket, took a deep breath and pushed his fingers into a crack between the stones.

Roland pulled himself up enough to get one foot into another crack in the stone wall, then found a hand grip higher up. Soon Roland was halfway between the ground and the window—and much too scared to look down.

The big blocks of stone that made up the wall were rough. This made it easier to find things to hold on to, but the stone was also cold and damp, which made it slippery. Right near the top of the wall, Roland's right hand suddenly slipped clean out. He let out a short scream but somehow held on with everything else and didn't fall.

"Nearly there," Roland said when his heartbeat finally slowed down. He stretched his fingers and just managed to reach the ledge below the window.

Another half push and he could grab one of the bars and use it to pull himself up.

"Got it, Nudge," Roland yelled with delight. "We've made it."

Roland now had two hands around the bars of the window and could pull himself up far enough to look out. He felt brave enough now to look down at the floor of the lockup. It was a terrifying distance below. Roland was amazed he had managed to climb so high.

Looking out through the grate, Roland realized that he and Nudge were high up in one of the castle's north towers. The window was just above the walkway that ran

along the top of the inner castle wall, and it gave a good view down to the bailey.

Roland could see that most people had fled the bailey or were standing behind the chapel wall. The elephant handler had returned. He was holding the leash and raising his whip. This time, though, the animal simply refused to move no matter how hard the leash was pulled.

Roland could tell even from way up high that the handler didn't want to use the whip. The man gave the elephant a couple of very gentle slaps but it just shook its head, flapped its ears, growled, then turned away.

Soon Roland noticed Hector walking out from behind the chapel wall.

"Give that to me," he shouted at the elephant handler. "What's needed here is a hero, not a coward."

Hector walked around the wine barrels, grabbed the whip and lashed the elephant as hard as he could. A horrible sound bounced around the castle walls as the leather whip hit the thick gray skin of the elephant's trunk and body.

"Stop, stop," yelled the handler as the elephant groaned, then squealed like a pig.

"Oh, Nudge, the poor animal."

Suddenly the elephant lifted its trunk high above its head. Its ears shot outward, its tail lifted and it charged three or four steps forward, its long tusks just missing Hector and the handler. They both ran as fast as they could back behind the chapel wall.

Although the mighty tusks missed

Hector and the handler, they did hit two of the wine barrels. The elephant was suddenly surrounded by pools of red wine that looked like blood.

What happened next surprised Roland— and everyone else. The elephant stuck its trunk into the pools of wine and noisily slurped them dry.

All the wine disappeared in just a few moments. The elephant stood still for a while, then started to look unsteady on its feet. It let out a mighty burp, then charged across the bailey and smashed into the wall protecting Hector, the handler and the frightened crowd.

There was an almighty crash but the wall held up. There was more screaming as the elephant trumpeted mightily, then pushed its tusks against the wall and tried to push it over.

Roland could see the wall begin to bend. Soon there was a tusk sticking right through the wooden slats, and the wall looked ready to fall.

Eight

In the Lockup

In desperation, the constable called in the royal archers. As the elephant readied to charge the wall again, they set their arrows and started pulling back their bowstrings.

The elephant moved away, as if it knew it was in danger, but suddenly the archers hesitated.

"I command you to halt," yelled King John from a window in the royal suites high above the chapel. "My elephant—my magnificent creature from the other side of the world—is a gift from Notjohn. You can't possibly harm it. It would be a horrible insult to my brother."

"Then what should we do, Your Majesty?" the constable yelled back. "How can we make sure the elephant doesn't squash someone?"

"We'll need to ask an expert," said King John. "Find me Lord Urbunkum!"

A short time later the constable arrived, pulling Lord Urbunkum along by the arm. "We found him, Your Majesty, under his bed."

"I was feeling a little low, Your Majesty," said Lord Urbunkum, "so I lay on my bed. Then I felt even lower, so I thought I should lie under it. But I'm here now and, and, and . . . and I'll do whatever I can to help. But I think it is best that I do it from on top of a wall. I find that reasoning works best from a position of authority."

Lord Urbunkum quickly made his way up to the walk atop the castle's northern wall—well clear of the elephant—and began talking down to it in a firm voice.

"You've had your fun now. You've done some damage. Nobody is blaming you, but it is time to go back to your pen. Returning of your own free will is an act that will make you a better person, er, elephant. You've got to decide what you want out of life and how you want others to judge you. . . ."

The elephant looked up and seemed to be listening. When Lord Urbunkum had finished, it lifted its trunk and sprayed him

with a mist of red wine, spit and elephant snot.

Lord Urbunkum blushed a deep scarlet and put his hands on his large stomach.

"I still feel off-color, Your Majesty," he said with a whimper. "Normally something like this wouldn't be a problem—I'm an expert on dragons, as you know—but I'm feeling very poorly and I need to return to my room."

Seconds later Lord Urbunkum was gone and the elephant was running wonkily around the bailey, turning every so often to again charge the wooden wall. Luckily, the guards had propped the wall up with more wood and it somehow managed to stay upright.

Roland could only watch from on high through the grated window. He wished he could help—even more so when he saw one of the squires race out of a doorway and into the bailey.

The squire, dressed in armor, was shouting at the elephant and trying to push it back toward its pen with his shield. But with just a tiny shove, the elephant squashed the squire in armor against a stone wall. It made a horrible sound, like a bug being crushed.

Two other squires ran out to grab the young man in the flattened armor. "Smithy," one of them called out as they bravely carried him past the elephant and ran toward the palace forge. "Smithy, help us cut him out. Quick!"

Three ladies had also rushed to help the squashed squire. They now found themselves stranded between the elephant and the only doorway that would lead them to safety. The elephant had them trapped and was letting out a deep rumbling sound. Its ears stuck out, its tail lifted and it looked ready to charge, even if its legs were still wobbly.

When Roland saw the three women he realized straightaway who the middle one was. Her pointed wimple had fallen almost completely off her head, showing her long red hair.

"Lady Mary, it's Lady Mary! We've got to help, Nudge, we've got to help."

Roland knew he had to escape, even if escaping was against all the rules. "Anyway, Nudge, how much more trouble can we be in?"

Roland pushed himself against the bars to see if he was slim enough to slip through. He breathed in as hard as he could, and Nudge did too. Roland pushed and pushed and . . . suddenly he and Nudge fell onto the stone walkway above the northern wall.

Without thinking exactly how he was going to help, Roland scooped Nudge back into his top pocket and ran down a set of stairs toward the three trapped women. He burst into the bailey . . . and— to even his own surprise—sprinted right through the elephant's legs. Seconds later he was facing the biggest creature he had ever seen.

King John watched from his window. He was just about to call back the archers to try to save the women when Roland appeared. Even though the boy looked unbelievably small next to the elephant, something made the King wait. He could see that while the trapped women were covering their faces and trying to squeeze into the corner, the thin redheaded boy was looking the elephant straight in the eye.

Even from on high, the King could
make out the determined look in that
young face as he tried to stare down the
huge animal. He could see too that instead
of putting his hands up to protect his face,
the boy had his hands by his side. He
seemed to be pushing his chest out toward
the elephant.

The elephant raised its trunk and let out the most amazing noise, somewhere between the blaring of trumpets and a human scream. The massive animal once more tensed and prepared to charge.

"That's the new page, isn't it?" said the King, squinting to get a better view as he yelled down to the constable. "Didn't you lock him up?"

"I thought I did, Your Majesty."

"Not very well, it seems. And I fear, Constable, that he's not going to be able to beat an elephant."

Nine

The Showdown

The elephant started to move slowly and unsteadily toward Roland. There was no doubt in anybody's mind that it could squash Roland in one blink and trample the three women in another.

There were screams and gasps but Twofold Castle's newest page didn't take a step backward. With his bottom lip stuck out and his eyes peering straight into those of the elephant, Roland instead started to walk forward.

Everyone held their breath as the elephant lowered its tusks and then swung its trunk right near Roland's face. Roland ducked but he didn't lift his hands to protect himself. He stood straight back up, with his arms pinned back and with his chest pushed out toward the huge animal.

As Roland took another step forward, the elephant did the same until they were almost nose to nose—or nose to trunk. Roland looked smaller and thinner than ever; the tusks looked large enough to poke right through his body if the elephant took just one more step forward. But Roland stood firm with his legs straight and his chest out.

Suddenly, with a grunt that echoed around the castle walls, the elephant lifted its right front leg—and moved it backward. It was only a half step, but it was soon followed by another half step in the same direction. The elephant was moving away from the three women, reversing toward its pen.

As the elephant slowly moved backward, Roland moved forward, his tiny steps now mirroring those of the huge beast. Once or twice it looked like the elephant was going to stop, but, after a pause here and there, it kept retreating.

When the elephant was finally in its pen the handler ran from behind the wall and closed the big wooden door, then slid the beam into place. He jammed the handle of his whip into the eyelet at the top so that the beam couldn't slide out.

"Success!" yelled someone in the crowd. Soon there was cheering all around as people moved out from behind the wall. Some ran toward Roland, others to the three women.

"Well done, Roland," shouted Lady Mary. "You saved us, and all on your own."

Lady Mary moved forward to give her special page a huge hug, but Lord Urbunkum suddenly reappeared and blocked the way.

"Calm down, calm down, everyone," he chirped above the noise of the crowd. "Fortunately the elephant listened to what I said and saw reason. I'm going to be modest about it, of course, but everyone should be aware that the big beast stopped its evil romp all because of me and my expert techniques."

Roland heard a sigh behind him, then a quiet and gentle voice said, "Isn't there some nonsense spoken in the world!"

Roland turned around and noticed it was the elephant handler.

"Hello, young page," the handler said. "You're the real hero. I've never seen anything like that in my life. How did you do it?"

Roland had another of his hunches. This was the kindly soul who didn't want to whip his animal, even when it wouldn't return to its pen. This man could definitely be trusted.

"You mustn't tell anyone this, Mr. Handler, but in my

top pocket I have a mouse. And he was sticking his face out of my surcoat and looking straight at the elephant."

The elephant handler responded with a strange look on his face. "I won't tell a soul, I promise. But surely you know that it's just a story that elephants are scared of mice?"

Roland looked down at the ground and started to feel sick. "Really?"

"Yes, it's a fiction, invented by minstrels to make people laugh. The truth is that elephants can just tread on anything that's worrying them, including mice—and pages. They probably can't even see something as small as a mouse."

Roland could feel the backs of his legs shaking. "Then why did the elephant walk backward if it wasn't afraid of my pet mouse, Nudge?"

"I think the elephant was surprised and impressed by your determination," said the handler with a laugh. "When I saw you sticking out your bottom lip and refusing to run away, even when the elephant swung its trunk at you, I thought: I'd probably go back to my pen for a little boy that brave, too."

At that moment, somebody moved out of the shadows next to the wall where Roland and the handler were standing.

"A mouse, hey?" came a snarl. "A mouse, s-s-s-s. The constable will love to hear this. So will the King, I'm sure."

"Leave him alone," shouted the elephant handler, but Hector was already gone. Roland felt as if he was going to throw up.

Soon Hector and the constable were walking toward Roland.

"Roland Wright," said the constable in his strictest, scariest voice, his bald head glinting in the sun and his huge eyebrows bouncing up and down. "You've let the elephant out, which is serious enough, then you escaped, which is also against the rules. Now I hear that you have a mouse as well."

"And he's a nasty little boy, too," said Hector. "That alone is a good enough reason to send him home, *s-s-s-s.*"

The constable turned to Hector. "Sending him home is not my decision—and it is certainly not yours, young Hector. The King personally invited this Roland Wright to Twofold Castle, so the matter should be decided by His Majesty himself."

The constable grabbed Roland by the sleeve. The next thing Roland knew, he was locked in another small room—and this one had no window. A short while later the door opened, there was yet another hand on Roland's arm and he was marched into the Great Hall.

King John was seated on an enormous throne, surrounded by guards. The King looked far bigger and more important than he had looked out in the bailey. He also looked far less kind and gentle.

"Master Wright," the King said, rubbing

his beard. "I hear you have a mouse, which I must admit doesn't concern me that much. Queen Margaret has to get over her fears. But far more seriously, Hector says it was you who let the elephant out. Is there any reason I shouldn't believe one of my most senior pages?"

Roland tried to say "You shouldn't believe him because he hates me. I didn't let out the elephant." But the words just fell silently out of Roland's mouth and landed at his feet.

"It was Lord Urbunkum who got the elephant back in, Your Majesty," said Hector. "You heard him yourself. And of course my own effort with the whip helped too, *s-s-s-s*. It weakened the elephant and taught it who was in charge.

"So rescuing us from the elephant was nothing to do with Roland. And even if this boy—this dirty little redhead—did have something to do with it, *s-s-s-s,* he would have been only undoing what he did in the first place."

The King looked at Roland. "I'm only going to ask you one time, young man. Did you let the elephant out?"

Again Roland was so scared he seemed unable to make a sound. He knew that if he didn't speak he was going to be locked up or sent home. But no words would come out of his mouth.

Roland had been in the royal household for just two days. He had seen very little of the castle and now, when he was finally meeting the King face to face, it was in the worst possible way. Roland was not going to be a proper page, or a squire, or a knight. He wasn't going to make his father and his brother proud. It was so unfair.

Ten

The King Decides

"**W**ell," said King John, "since Roland seems unable to talk, perhaps Hector could tell us why the new page let the elephant out."

"Because . . ." Hector paused to think. "Because, *s-s-s-s,* because he's poor, Your Majesty, and poor children can't be trusted."

Hector scratched his head as if working out what to say next. "He was probably going to eat it. Yes, *s-s-s-s,* that's it, he thought if something that big escaped and had to be shot, then everyone would feast on it. He wanted to eat elephant because he is angry that you don't feed him cockentrice every night. Yes, Your Majesty, *s-s-s-s*, that's why he let the elephant out."

Hector walked up to Roland, who tensed, thinking he was about to be punched. Instead, Hector reached into Roland's pocket and turned to the King.

"Look, Your Majesty, here's the iron bolt from the gate, *s-s-s-s*, still in his pocket. What more proof could you possibly need?"

"Guards, seize this young boy right now," the King said. As men moved in from each side, the King took off his crown, held it in his hands and looked straight into Roland's eyes.

"Do you have any idea how disappointed I am, young Roland Wright? I gave you this marvelous opportunity to make something of your life and you've done this in return. My elephant—a gift from my brother—was nearly killed by the archers because you let it out. It could just as easily have squashed people to death, all because of your stupid deed."

Roland could feel tears sliding down his cheeks as the King spoke.

"And imagine being angry, young Roland, because I don't feed you cockentrice every night. How ungrateful. I'm going to have you shipped home forthwith, before you even receive your first proper page uniform. You should be pleased I don't have you flogged first or sent to the dungeon to see what sort of food some people have to eat."

Hector broke into a wide smile. He started humming to himself, although even Hector's humming was also mixed with hissing.

"Hmmm-hmmm-hmmm, *s-s-s-s, s-s-s-s,* hmmm-hmmm-hmmm, *s-s-s-s,* hmmm-hmmm-hmmm, *s-s-s-s.*"

The humming and hissing stopped suddenly when three people burst into the room.

"Well, if it isn't Humphrey Humphrey," said Hector. "And fat little Morris, *s-s-s-s,* the teller of tall tales. And . . . who is this other person?"

"Your Majesty, Your Majesty," Humphrey said in a trembling voice. "I know I shouldn't interrupt, shouldn't interrupt." Humphrey danced around and his long straw-colored hair shook. "But, but . . ."

King John held up his hand and

boomed over the top of Humphrey's tiny voice: "It's an extraordinary day when a page who is asked a question by a king won't answer, and another who hasn't been asked a single thing bursts in and starts talking."

The room was now completely quiet as the King said in his sternest voice, "If you haven't a good reason for coming in here, young Humphrey, you'll be in just as much trouble as Roland."

"There's a sentry who must explain something, explain something, Your Majesty," said Humphrey.

"Surely it can wait," the King said impatiently.

"No, it c-a-n't," butted in Morris, who was so worried about what he was doing that his voice almost disappeared before the end of his first short sentence. The King's angry gaze switched to Morris and everyone nervously waited to see what would happen next.

"Well, come up here, sentry," the King said briskly, "and tell us what you have to say."

"Your Majesty," said the sentry nervously as he removed his helmet and smoothed his red and blue surcoat over his shirt of mail. "I have been on guard duty at the western tower lookout since the early morn. When I finished, Your Majesty, I told another sentry what I had seen—and these boys heard me and begged me to come and tell you, Your Majesty, the same story."

"Out with it, man," said the King, now losing his temper. "Be quick and get straight to the point or you'll regret it."

The sentry now had an even more worried tremor in his voice. And he spoke even more softly. "A few hours ago, Your Majesty . . ."

"Louder!" snapped the King. "And I want fewer 'Your Majestys' and more facts."

"Yes, Your Maj— I mean no, Your Maj— Anyway, I saw a page sneaking around. He was looking about, as if to make sure no one saw what he was doing—but I could still see him from up on high because I was looking into the bailey while I adjusted my crossbow.

"When the boy thought no one was looking he pulled the bolt out from the top of the sliding beam on the elephant's gate, gave the beam a bit of a push and then ran into the shadows as fast as he could."

"Are you telling us anything new?" asked the King. "We know that a page let the elephant out, and we know who that boy is."

"I'm sorry, Your Maj— I didn't know that," said the sentry, who started to back out of the room. "I'm sorry for wasting your time."

"Wait, sentry," said the King. "Just so there are no mistakes made, perhaps you could point out the boy you saw."

"Yes, of course, Your Maj—" said the sentry. He looked very closely at Roland, then said in a strong, clear voice, "That's him!"

Humphrey and Morris turned almost white and Roland was ready to throw himself on the ground and scream. But as he mouthed the words "That's him!," the sentry spun around and pointed straight at Hector.

"And after he undid the gate," the sentry continued in a much stronger and more confident manner, "I saw him sneak up behind another boy and put the bolt in his pocket."

"And then," added the sentry, who had begun to enjoy telling his story in front of such an important audience, "the boy, the one who opened the gate, went up and talked to the elephant handler, who quickly left the bailey."

The King rubbed his beard. "I see. That's why the elephant man insisted I had called for him. Guards—release Roland, and put Hector in the stocks straightaway."

Roland closed his eyes and sighed the deepest sigh of relief he had ever sighed.

"Fetch Roland his new page uniform," the King added. "And tell the cooks that tonight we will have a cockentrice in honor of the tiny boy who stared down the biggest animal to walk the earth. Yes, we will have a huge cockentrice, with fire coming out of its mouth, in honor of our newest, bravest page: Roland Wright."

"And his mouse, Nudge," said Roland, who suddenly found his voice had returned, and didn't stop to think that he was standing before a king and had no right to say anything unless asked a question. Worse still, as Roland said it, he reached into his pocket and pulled Nudge out into full view of everyone in the room.

The constable, the other pages and everyone else looked aghast. Roland immediately realized what he had done and was now holding his breath in shock.

The King scrunched up his eyes and looked set to jump out of his throne, but he suddenly relaxed. Everyone else did likewise.

"And his mouse," King John repeated in a gentle voice. "What did you say the name was?"

"It's Nudge, Your Majesty. He's a boy."

"Well, then, we owe a big thank-you to Nudge as well. I am going to name him the official mouse of Twofold Castle."

"Flaming catapults, Your Majesty . . ."
Roland was stunned, but after a short
while he started to smile. At first it was a
small smile, but it grew larger and larger
and larger. Soon he was smiling more
widely than he had ever smiled before.

Roland thanked King John four times
in a row. He bowed as low as he could at
least five times and asked if Humphrey and
Morris could come to the banquet too.

"I don't see why not," answered the
King. "I think all the pages should come.
All the pages, except one."

There was a huge hooray from the
pages in the room, and from Lady Mary,
who had walked in to find Roland. When
the cheering finally died down, Roland
walked out into the bailey. Nudge was now
on his right shoulder, sniffing the air with
his twitchy pink nose.

As Roland moved out of the shadows
and into the daylight, he could see Hector
was already in the stocks, his head and

hands clamped in tightly, the sun beating down on his face.

"I won't forget this, *s-s-s-s,* you horrible, horrible poor boy," Hector yelled when he saw Roland. "I'll get you b—"

Roland was sure the word that Hector wanted to say was "back." It never came out, though, because at that exact moment a woman threw a piece of rotten fruit at Hector. It hit him straight in the mouth.

"You should do the same," the woman said to Roland. "What with him telling lies about you and everything."

Roland wasn't going to throw anything at Hector. He remembered something that Sir Gallawood had told him, about being true to yourself, about doing as well as you possibly could in every situation, and about behaving justly, nobly and never selfishly— no matter what the other person did.

That was how a good knight behaved, and that was how Roland wanted to behave. There was nothing to be gained by throwing a rotting tomato at Hector, though Roland did admit to himself it might have been fun.

Besides, Roland felt too happy to do something so mean-spirited: too happy for himself, and too happy for Nudge. Now they could both stay at the castle. Roland just wished his father and brother were here so he could tell them of his and Nudge's adventures. He wished he could share it all with his neighbor from the village, Jenny

Winterbottom. After all, she had played her own little part in helping Roland win his place at the castle.

Roland turned away from Hector and slowly looked around the bailey, finally stopping at the elephant's pen. He stared into the big eyes of the magnificent animal and was sure he saw one of them wink at him.

Roland smiled at the elephant and then noticed the drawbridge was being opened so the King could go on a hunt. Roland looked out across the moat, over the fields and into the distant hills.

"Roland Wright," he said to himself as he clutched the neatly folded red and blue uniform the King had personally presented. "Roland Wright, brand-new page. And his mouse, Nudge, by Royal Appointment."

"   ," added Nudge proudly.

Acknowledgments

The author would like to dedicate this book to his sons, William, James, and Daniel, all of whom have provided feedback and inspiration in Roland's developing story, and to his wife, Carolyn Walsh, without whom none of it would have happened.

Others have read the manuscript and offered opinions I value: Graham Harman; David Mason-Cox; Alexa Moses; Sharon "No Relation" Davis; Lachlan and Joshua Coady; Glenn Morrison; Debbie Vermes; my brother, Damian; and my parents, Pedr and Dolores.

Many publishing people have made special efforts on behalf of "our little knight." They include Zoe Walton, Kimberley Bennett, Justin Ractliffe, Yae Morton, and Françoise Bui. Lastly, thanks to Gregory Rogers for again bringing my words to life so vividly with his delightful illustrations.

About the Author

Tony Davis has always worked with words. He has been a book publisher, a magazine editor, and a newspaper writer. In recent years he has been a full-time book author—his most difficult but exciting job yet.

Tony has long been interested in knights and armor, and the legends and stories of the Middle Ages. His enthusiasm for the period comes through clearly in the world of Roland Wright.

When he is not putting words on paper (or screens), Tony is playing football or cricket in the backyard with his three sons, strumming a guitar, reading, hiking, or listening to music on his stereo, iPod, or hand-cranked 78-rpm record player.

About the Illustrator

Gregory Rogers studied fine art at the Queensland College of Art in Australia and has illustrated a large number of educational and trade children's picture books. He won the Kate Greenaway Medal for his illustrations in *Way Home*.

His first wordless picture book, *The Boy, The Bear, The Baron, The Bard,* was selected as one of the *New York Times* Ten Best Illustrated Children's Books of the Year and received numerous other awards and nominations. He also illustrated *Midsummer Knight,* the companion to *The Boy, The Bear, The Baron, The Bard*.

Coming Soon

Roland Wright's knightly adventures continue in

Roland Wright #3
At the Joust

Here's an excerpt from Chapter One:

Roland Wright couldn't decide which was worse: the clanging great longsword that kept crashing on his helmet, rattling his teeth and threatening to cleave his head in two, or the hiccups.

Whenever he tried to defend himself, exactly the same thing happened. "H'uppp!" then *clang!*

He should never have eaten those grapes. And he should never have tried to fight this knight.

They were both using longswords, large heavy weapons that were held with two hands, meaning neither fighter had a shield.

Roland pointed his leading foot toward his target: the very top of the knight's helmet. He turned his back foot sideways for better balance. He kept his body straight and made sure his weight was on the balls of his feet. He changed his grip, holding his longsword

tightly just behind the cross-guard with his stronger hand, his left hand.

But as his blade swooped, Roland was hit yet again with the pommel of the knight's blade—*doinggg!*—and found himself lying on the ground, looking up at a knight raising his longsword and preparing to bring it down like a spear.

For the first time, Roland was scared.

He closed his eyes, fearing that his last word on earth would be "H'uppp!"